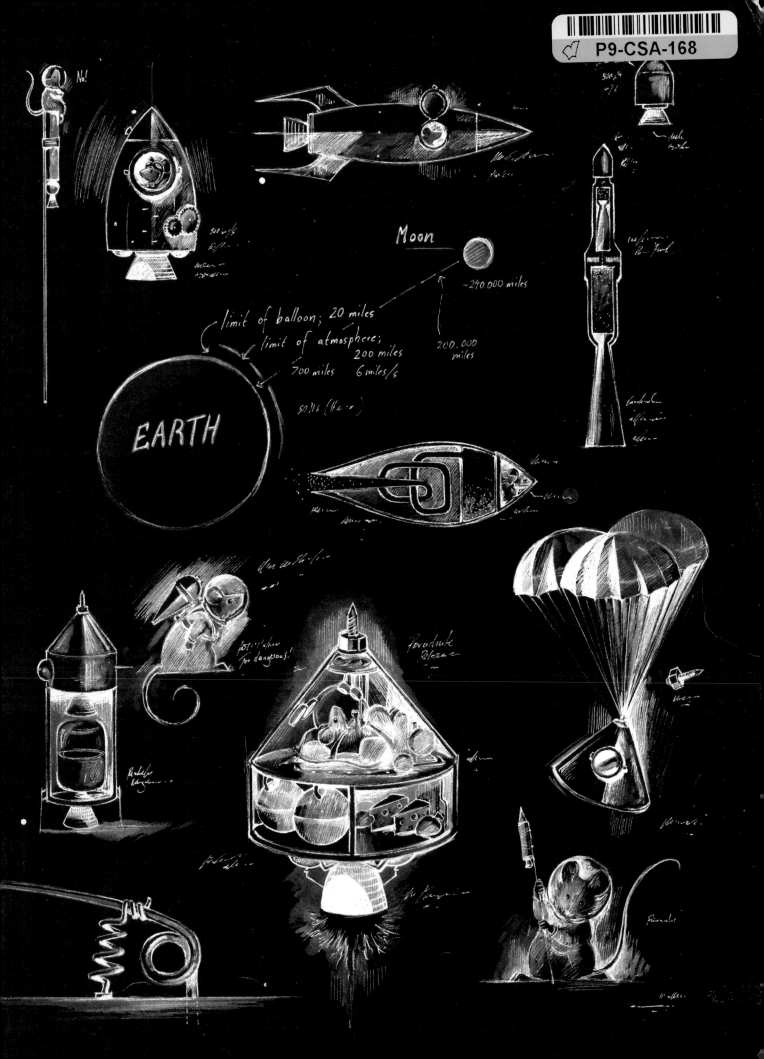

Foreword

Once upon a time, not so long ago, children played with toy spaceships and began to dream of going to the moon. Adults also found the idea intriguing, especially engineers and scientists who understood machinery and mathematics. The problem was, no one knew exactly how to do it, or even precisely where in space the moon was located; and no one knew if anyone could survive such a trip.

This imaginative retelling of the first journey to the moon is true, mostly. The challenges and problem solving; the inventiveness and dedication; the tests and failures and, yes, the tragedy and ultimately the successes all occurred much as they are depicted here. Even more than the words, the richly detailed illustrations reveal how the first space farers cleverly worked their way through myriad puzzles of spacecraft and space suit design and managed to land on the moon.

For those born after 1965 or so, this story of indomitable will and ingenuity may not be familiar, so *Armstrong* tells it anew. This book will delight space cadets of all ages who dream big dreams and commit to achieving them, as did everyone who figured out how to go to the moon and back.

Ad astra per aspera. (Through hardships to the stars.)

Valerie Neal
Chair, Space History Department
Curator, Human Spaceflight
National Air and Space Museum
Smithsonian Institution

ARMSTRONG

The New York Times

NEW YORK, MONDAY, JULY 21, 1969

MEN WALK ON MOON

ASTRONAUTS LAND ON PLAIN; COLLECT ROCKS, PLANT FLAG

Voice From Moon:
'Eagle Has Landed'

A Powdery Surface
Is Closely Explored

FSC
www.fsc.org
MIX
Paper from
responsible sources
FSC® C002795

Torben Kuhlmann

ARMSTRONG

The Adventurous Journey of a Mouse to the Moon

Translated by David Henry Wilson

North
South

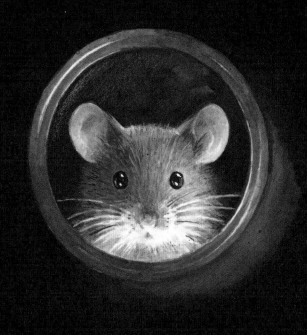

The Stargazer

A small paw turned the little wheel of a gigantic telescope, and a tiny bundle of gray fur peered through the iron tube full of glass lenses. Now the picture of the starry sky was perfectly clear.

"Incredible!" murmured the little mouse.

Every night the mouse observed the night sky. He was particularly fascinated by the moon. At first it hung in the sky, fat and round. But then it became thinner and thinner, until there was nothing to be seen except a narrow crescent. The following night, it had disappeared completely.

The little mouse recorded every detail of his observations.

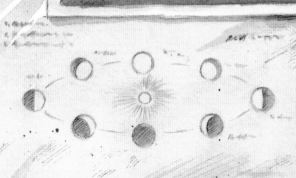

All the mice in the town met regularly at a secret place. There were boxes and cartons piled right up to the ceiling, and their contents made this place into an absolute paradise for mice. The little mouse set off to meet his fellow mice there.

He proudly showed the others everything he had discovered through his telescope.

"The moon is a giant ball of stone!"

With shining eyes and a voice that trembled with excitement, he told them all he knew.

"The light from the sun is what makes the moon shine and . . ."

The little mouse broke off in midsentence. He could see that nobody was listening. The other mice did not want to hear any more, because they believed something quite different. . . .

The Tale of the Big Cheese

For mice there is nothing more wonderful than cheese. Spicy or mild, creamy or hard with holes in it. Cheese runs a mouse's life. And so for the mice everything was crystal clear: the moon was made of cheese. How else could one explain it? The moon is a round ball and has holes in it. Sometimes it is as yellow as Gouda, then as white as Camembert, or even as reddish orange as Leicester. And now all of a sudden the moon is supposed to be a ball of stone?

The little mouse tried again and again to convince the other mice, and every day he reported his findings, but it was all in vain.

One night, the little mouse sat sadly on a box of Parmesan. He was all alone. The other mice had long since gone home. Pale moonlight shone through a small basement window, and it fell on his notes. And in the dim light he found something: somebody had sent him a letter. Not a big letter, such as humans would write. It was a mouse-sized letter. Quickly he opened it. Inside the envelope was an entrance ticket: *"Smithsonian?!"*

The mouse could not decipher anything else. But under this printed word was a paw-written message:

"You are right! Come and see me."

A Journey into the Past

"Nothing is too difficult for a clever mouse!" said the little
mouse with a smile. He had soon found out where the
mysterious letter had come from, and now he was on his way
to see his unknown pen pal. For a mouse that knew his way
around the world of humans, even long journeys were no
problem. He had decided to take the train. In his luggage he
had packed some cheese and his notes.

When no one was looking, he climbed onto a pile of
suitcases and jumped into a carriage. The guard blew his
whistle, and the train rumbled on its way.

"I wonder what I'll find there . . . ," murmured the four-
legged passenger.

NEW YORK

WASHINGTON, D.C.

"Wow!" cried the little mouse. His squeaky voice echoed through the cavernous rooms.

"A museum, full of human inventions!"

The little explorer trotted reverently through the hallway toward a staircase that led down to the basement. The rooms below were dusty and dark, and packed with relics from past times.

"Oh, look!" he squeaked to himself. Someone had done a chalk drawing on the wall portraying a little winged mouse. Below it was an arrow. The mouse followed the sign, and found himself standing in front of a mouse hole.

Flying Mice and Fantastic Adventures

The mouse hole led straight into a large room with a low ceiling. And what the little mouse saw there took his breath away. Flying machines, hang gliders, and all sorts of weird and wonderful apparatus hung from the ceiling or stood on the floor. It looked just like the human museum above. But these were mouse-flying machines.

"What *is* this place?" whispered the little mouse in awe.

"Here you can see the history of mouse aviation!" said a voice that echoed through the room. "How wonderful that you've come! So you got my message."

Out of the shadow of a large flying machine stepped an old gray mouse. He smoothed his stubbly whiskers, straightened his glasses, and very formally stretched out a paw to greet the little mouse. With his other front paw he leaned on a walking stick.

"I heard about your discoveries, and I thought this place might be of interest to you. You see, there was once a time when nothing was impossible for us mice. We traveled the world, and even learned how to fly. But at some time or another, mice became interested in other things. And gradually they forgot all about their flying ancestors."

The little mouse listened in amazement to the old mouse's tales.

He was fascinated. So there had been flying mice in the old days! And if a mouse could learn to fly then, maybe it was possible for a mouse to fly to the moon now.

"I shall be the first mouse on the moon!" he cried.

The next day, the little mouse traveled back to his hometown. His head was full of ideas and ambitious plans. The old mouse in the museum had given him lots of helpful advice.

"Study human knowledge. Some humans are really clever."

And so the mouse spent the next few weeks in the municipal libraries, and sometimes he even slipped into the university.

But he soon found out that the moon was a lot farther away than he had thought. And nothing and nobody had ever flown so high before. Higher than the clouds, higher even than the air one breathes. The moon circled in the icy, airless nothingness of space.

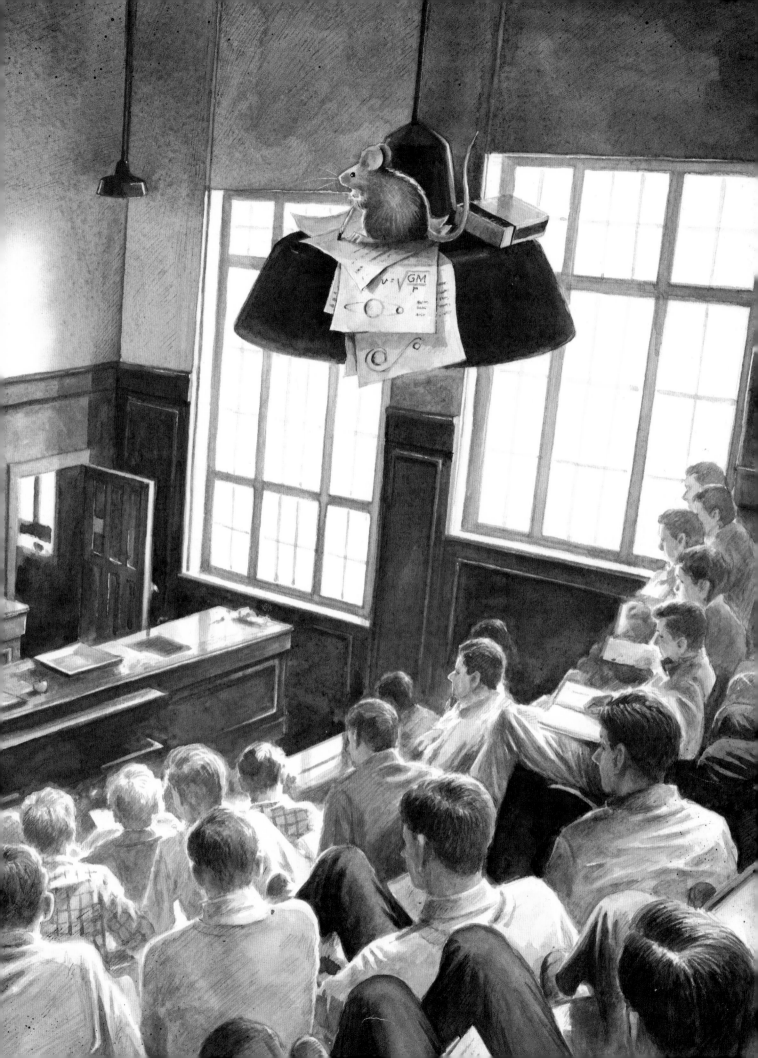

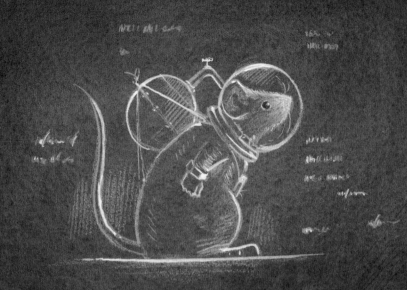

The Space Suit

"So many problems to be solved," sighed the little mouse, but he did not allow himself to be discouraged. The first step was to find a way in which he could simply survive in space. He would have to wrap himself up safe and warm, and take enough air in his luggage to be able to keep breathing.

"It could work!" he squeaked through his whiskers, and he made a little drawing.

Next he would need some building materials. A lot of building materials. And he already had a good idea how he could test his space suit. . . .

William Steelworks Inc.

William's Wrap

Classic Aluminum

FOIL

MATCHES

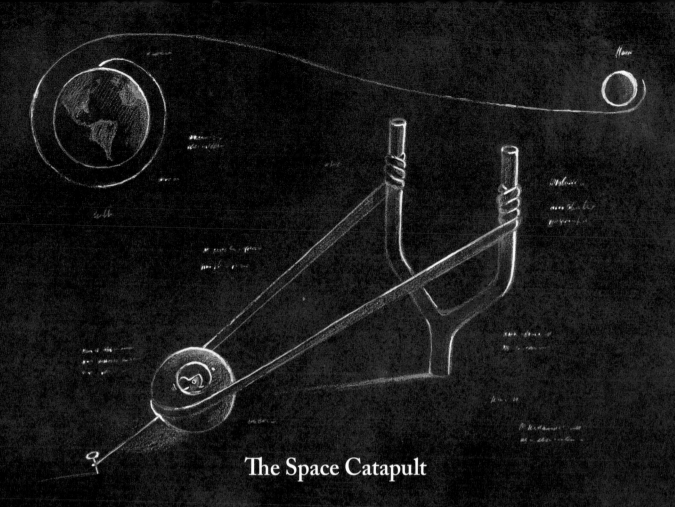

The Space Catapult

The space suit worked. The test was a complete success.
The mouse would be able to breathe in space just as he could
underwater. But the test must have given the goldfish the
shock of his life.

The next task was a lot more difficult.

"How can one get to fly so high—to take off from the
earth and fly to the moon? Balloon? Airplane?"

For days and days this question went round and round
the little mouse's brain. Perhaps it might work with a big
sling? Or some kind of catapult? Once again, he made a little
drawing.

"I need a strong metal container. And a lot of rubber
bands . . . or something like that."

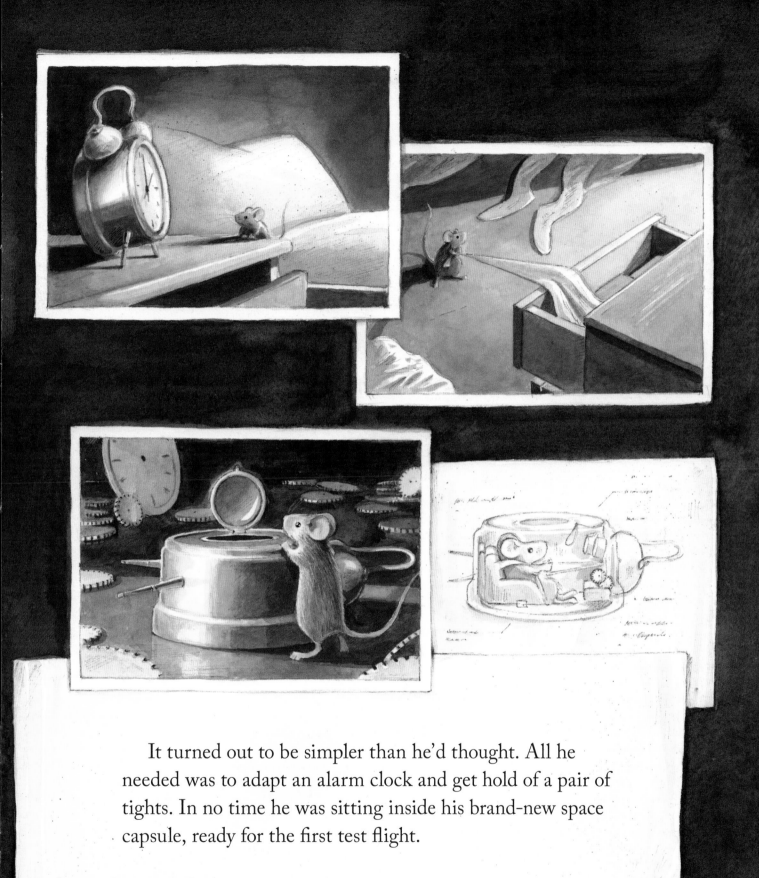

It turned out to be simpler than he'd thought. All he needed was to adapt an alarm clock and get hold of a pair of tights. In no time he was sitting inside his brand-new space capsule, ready for the first test flight.

With a quick pull, the little mouse released the anchor.
Boing! The elastic tights straightened to their full length
and catapulted pilot and space capsule high into the sky.
Everything was awhirl. The acceleration pushed the little
mouse hard against the pilot's seat.

"I'm flying!" he shouted, although he hadn't a clue
which way was up and which was down. The space capsule
zoomed in a high arc over the roofs and chimneys.

But inevitably the capsule began to lose impetus.

"Oh no . . . Have I stopped flying? I'm falling!" cried the
little mouse in dismay. With a great effort he bent forward
and pulled on a string. There was a *wheee* and a *whoosh*,
and a white cloth shot out of the back of the alarm clock,
putting a brake on the downward dive.

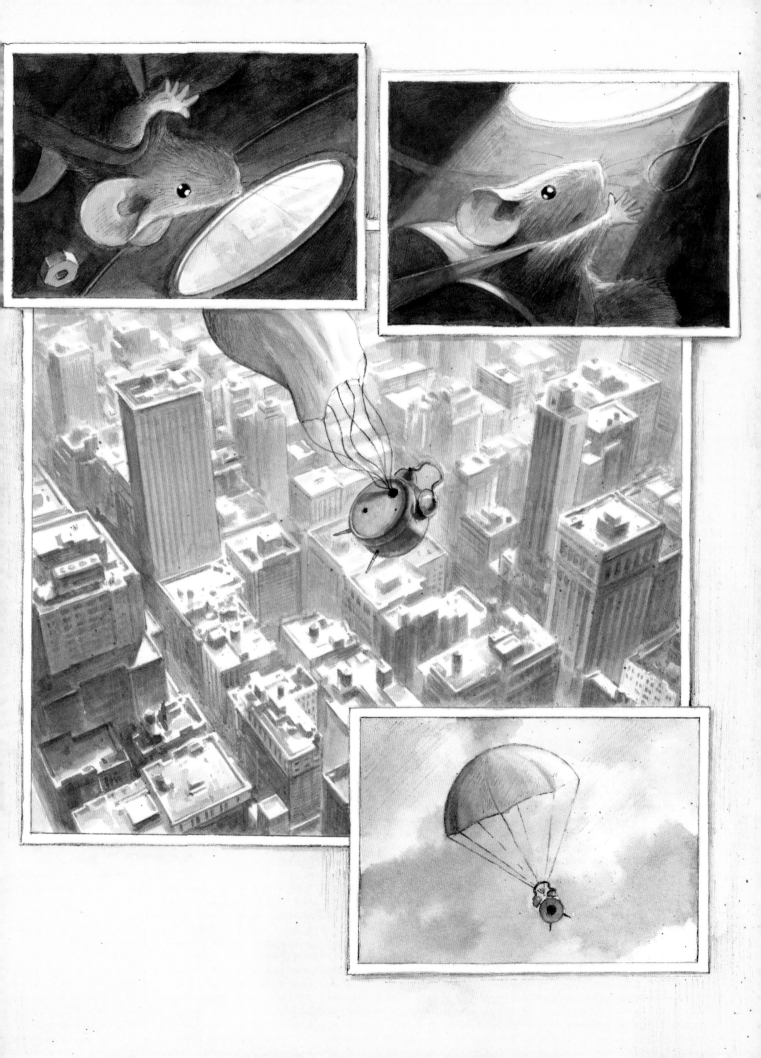

The Rocket Sled

"That was a disaster!" moaned the little mouse, sitting in his capsule. It was anything but simple to get back on solid ground. The alarm clock was still dangling high above the busy streets. The parachute had gotten tangled up in a cable. The little mouse tied a few strings together to make a long rope and climbed out of his open-air prison. One thing was certain: a catapult would never fire him up into space.

Night was falling when the mouse trudged home between the tall rows of houses. Suddenly there was a hissing and a flashing and a banging, and bright lights lit up the sky.

"Fireworks?!"

When he had recovered from the first shock, the little mouse looked for a suitable vantage point from which he could observe the colorful spectacle.

And then he had an idea. . . .

The little mouse fastened the last strap. The rocket was now firmly attached to the underside of the roller skate. All he needed was one more set of wings and a long ramp.

He was putting together the last few bits and pieces—the control column and the firing mechanism—when suddenly there was a loud crackle and sparks began to fly. With a terrible roar, the engine fired.

"Oh no, not now!"

The rocket sled shot forward. It hurtled across the room, spitting smoke and flames, and crashed into a pile of books and junk.

A cloud of thick black smoke billowed out of the windows.
The whole attic was in flames. At lightning speed, the fire cut
through the dry wooden beams. The notes and drawings on
the walls instantly turned to ashes. The terrified mouse could
rescue only one of his designs from the raging inferno.

Down in the street, sirens were wailing and men in big helmets were shouting to one another.

"What a catastrophe!" whispered the little mouse.

Everything had gone up in flames—all his notes, the rocket sled, and even his telescope. Sobbing his heart out, he crept away from the scene, sadly dragging behind him the one design that he had been able to save.

The giant telephone was not easy to use. The little mouse needed all his strength to dial the numbers. *Rrriiinnnggg.* There was a ringing sound, and then a familiar squeaky voice answered at the other end. It was the old mouse from the museum.

"I've heard what happened. Are you all right?" the old mouse asked in a worried tone.

The little mouse told him all about his adventures from his first attempt to fly, right through to the disaster with the rocket sled.

"You must take more care," the old mouse warned his young friend. "We mice can easily get hurt."

They talked for a long time.

"And one more thing. Be on the alert. The humans have got their eyes on you now."

The Rocket Mouse

The little mouse was still furious with himself for not having been more careful. Because in fact the rocket had worked perfectly. The engine was unbelievably powerful. It didn't need wings or wheels or anything like that. . . .

He wanted to try again. His rocket design looked extremely promising. And he had also found a new hideaway for himself. It had a fireplace and a chimney, which he could try out as a launching pad.

First, though, he needed to get some new parts, but his thieving expeditions were dangerous. Men in long coats and dark floppy hats were popping up and sniffing around all over the place. What the old mouse had said was true: humans were out hunting for the little thief and arsonist.

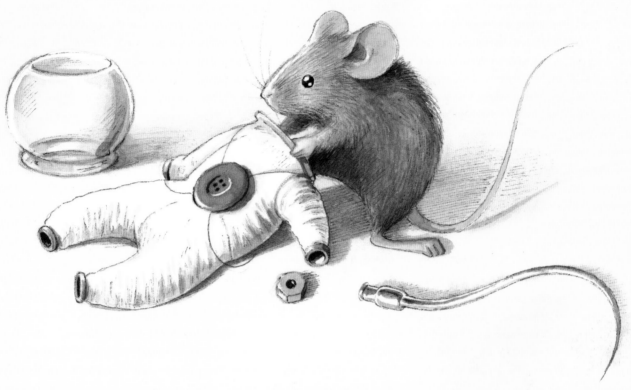

The rocket was almost ready. It stood there sparkling in
the soot-covered fireplace. A tower of silver cans, each with
its own engine. One by one he would fire them and shoot the
capsule up to heights that had never been reached before.

With a metallic click the top section snapped shut. All
ready for takeoff.

The little mouse slipped into his space suit. The rocket
was full of fuel. Cheese, bread, and water had been safely
stowed on board. The mouse reached for his space helmet.
Suddenly there was a rattling sound on the staircase leading
to his front door.

"Darn! The floppy hats!" moaned the mouse. The humans had found his hiding place. Panic-stricken, he raced back through the front door, skidded across the smooth floorboards, and reached the fireplace with seconds to spare.

Dogs came chasing after him, barking and growling, and the floppy hats shouted things he couldn't understand. He grabbed hold of his helmet, raced up the ladder, slammed the hatch behind him, and pressed a large red button.

The capsule groaned and began to shake. The pressure forced the little mouse back hard into his seat. He could scarcely move. With a loud hiss, the rocket shot up through the chimney shaft, and then through the chimney itself. A huge flame blazed from beneath the rocket, leaving a cloud of thick smoke behind it.

The floppy hats were left standing there, faces black with soot. They crowded together at the windows, pressed their noses flat against the glass, and watched the sparkling rocket fly upward, with the little astronaut on board. The mouse had escaped. But when they searched his hideaway, they found something else. . . .

The Journey to the Moon

The blue sky grew darker and darker, as if suddenly night
was falling. The stars were shining from the deep blackness
of the universe. Far below the mouse in his space capsule,
the continents of planet Earth whirled past, and the oceans
shone in the sunlight.

"Like a beautiful blue-green jewel," whispered the little
mouse admiringly.

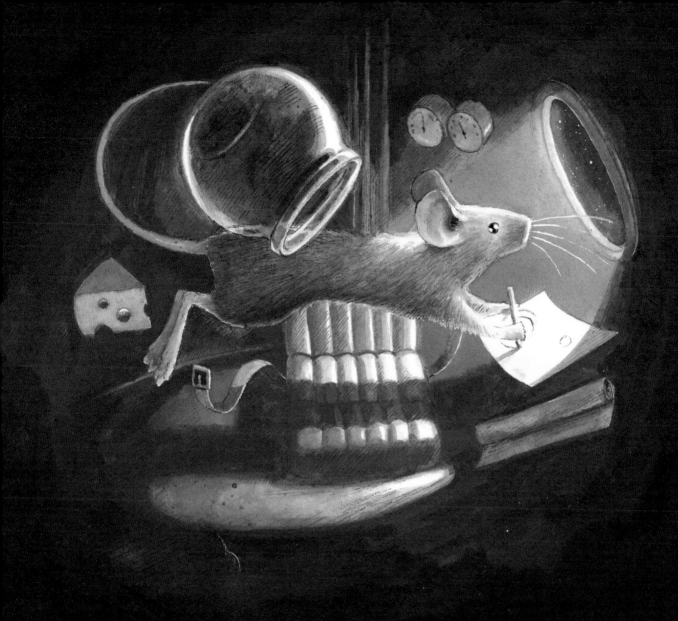

He released his safety belt. The force of the movement was no longer pressing him back into his seat. In fact it was the opposite. He now floated weightlessly around the little capsule, accompanied by his helmet and a few bits of cheese.

"Next stop, the moon!" he announced in a loud and cheerful voice, although there was no one to hear him.

He could see the moon through his peephole. Small and round, it hung in front of the starry sky. But as each day passed, it became bigger, and soon it no longer fit in the tiny window.

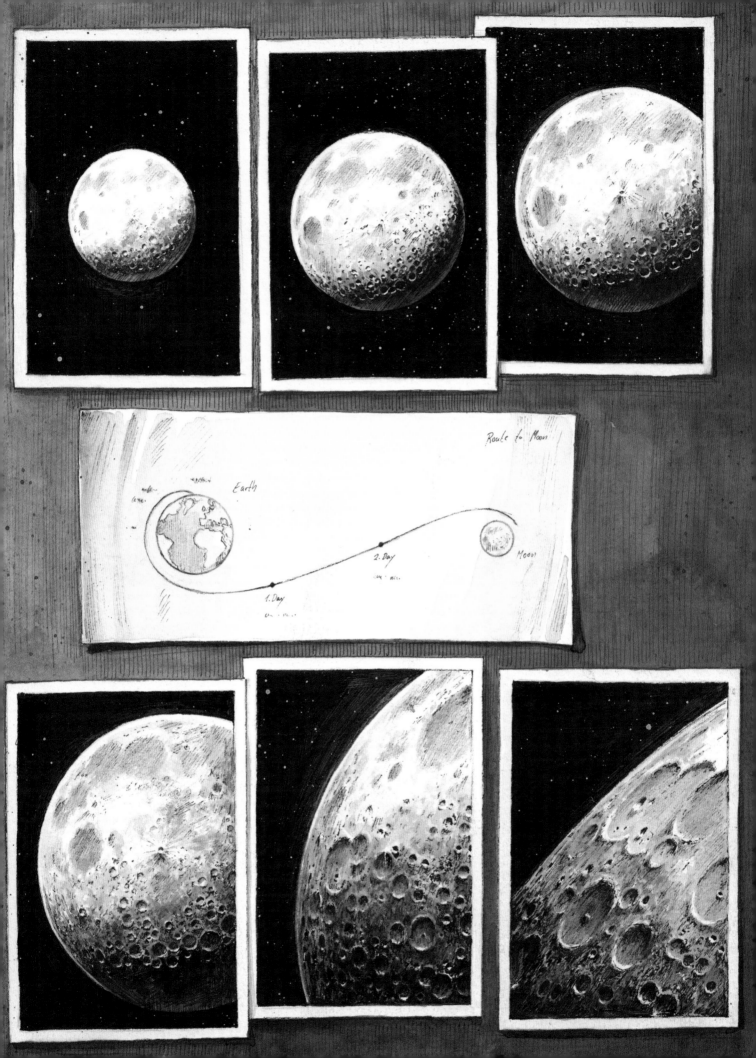

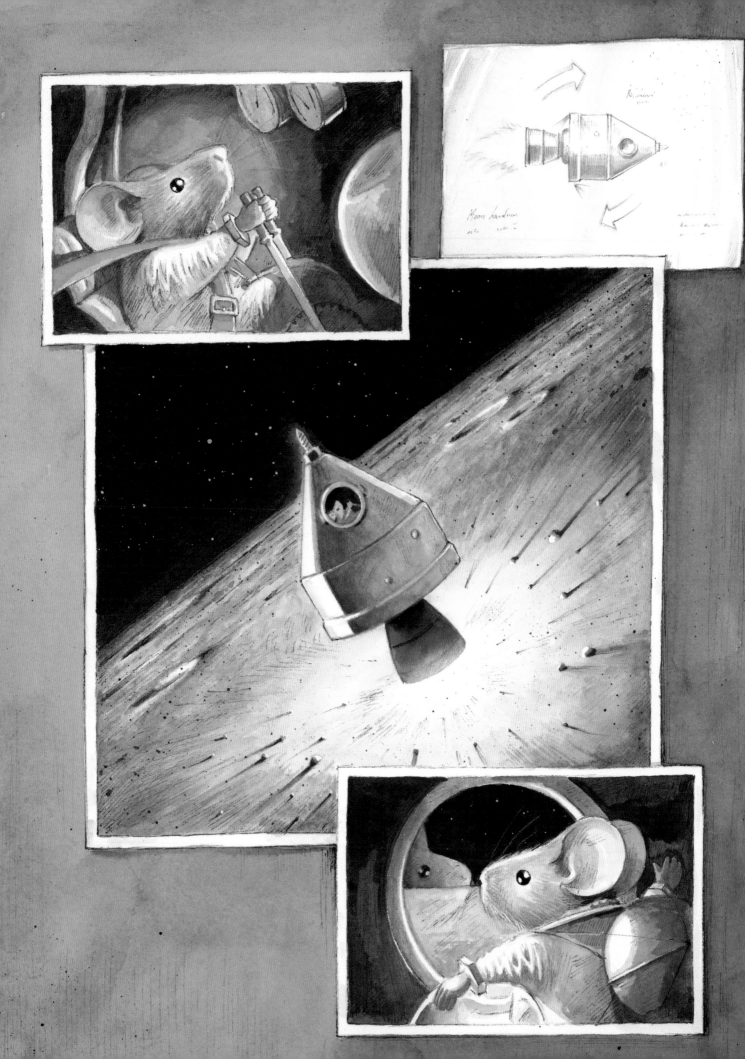

One Small Step for a Mouse

The little mouse's voyage through the dark void of space took three days. By now the moon was very large indeed. Its floury-white surface was covered with craters, some big and others small. They were really nothing like cheese holes! The little mouse floated into his pilot's seat and fastened his safety belt. He would begin his landing procedure shortly.

    The engine swirled up a cloud of gray dust. Then the space capsule landed, and with a beating heart and a marveling mind the little mouse unbolted the hatch.

With unexpected ease, the little space mouse bounced over the dusty surface of the moon. Tiny hops turned into giant leaps up here. He studied the craters all around the spot where he had landed, and he examined the moon rock.

"I'll take this piece of stone with me," he squeaked, "as evidence to show the other mice."

After many hours of research, he climbed back into his space capsule. Without a sound, the flying machine took off. Left behind were countless paw prints and one very special flag.

After three days, the little mouse returned to planet Earth.
He didn't need his rocket anymore. With a quiet hissing
sound, it freed itself and floated silently away. The tip of the
space capsule went plunging toward the earth and the capsule
began to glow.

The Return of the Moon Mouse

The space capsule—now somewhat blackened—slid down through the clouds on three red parachutes. Inside sat a very relieved little mouse.

"I'm home again!" he cried joyfully.

Bummmppp! The capsule hit the ground. The little mouse unfastened his safety belt and unbolted the hatch. Fresh air gushed into the capsule. He stuck his head through the round opening. And what he saw then moved him almost to tears. . . .

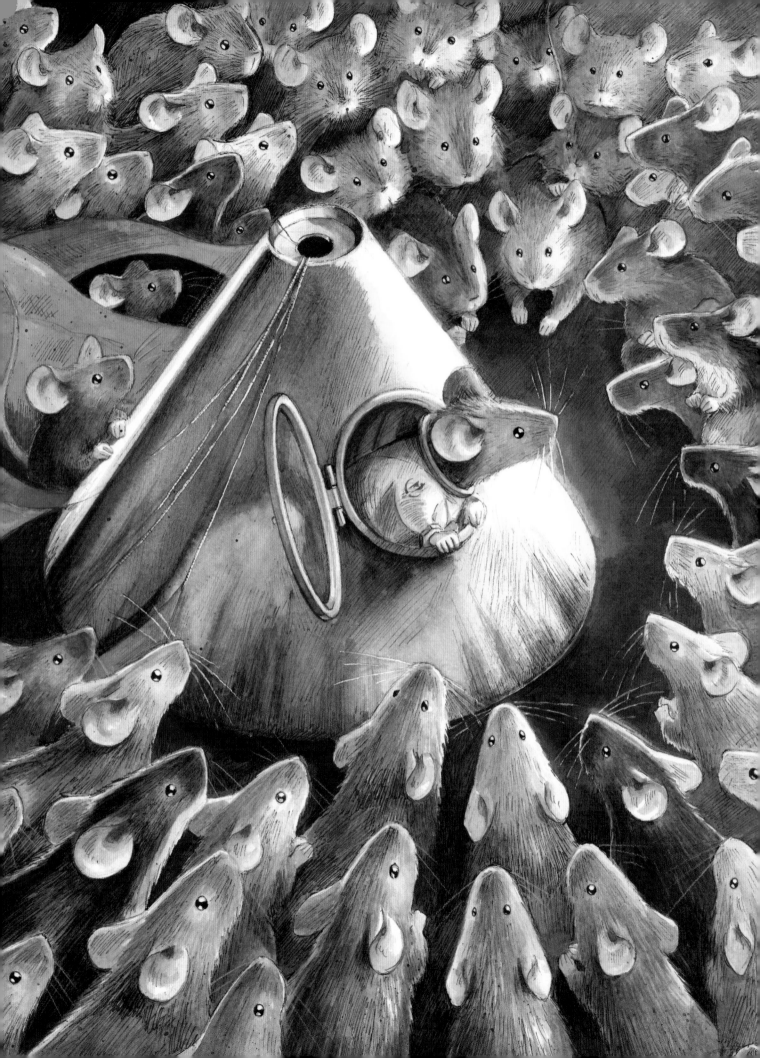

One Big Step for Mankind

The little mouse was very happy. His mission had been a complete success. It was not long before the story of his space adventure was being told to mice all over the country. There was not a mouse who now believed the moon was made of cheese.

And the humans? Most of them knew absolutely nothing about all the excitement in the mouse world. However, just a few were soon sitting with whirling brains over the mouse-sized rocket designs, and in due course they also came up with a wonderful plan.

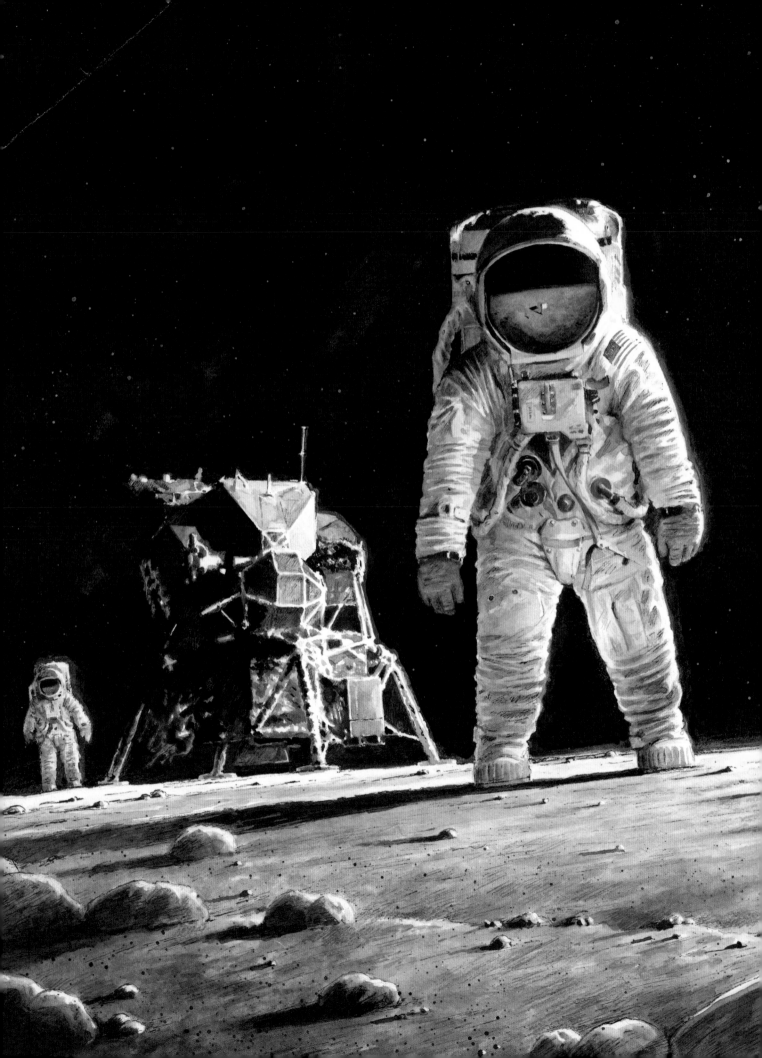

And so on July 21, 1969, the first human stepped onto the surface of the moon. But scarcely anyone knows what he found there.

"ARMSTRONG"
The First Moon Landing

TOP SECRET

Daily Record

UFO Sighting

Witness: "Tiny, Grey Passenge

Of course there were some who knew about the little moon mouse, and they named him Armstrong.

That way, he had the same name as the first man to step on the moon. And that meant that nobody could possibly give away the secret by accident. Because whenever anyone asked who had been the first to step on the moon, the answer was simply "Armstrong."

Moon Mouse
1955

The End

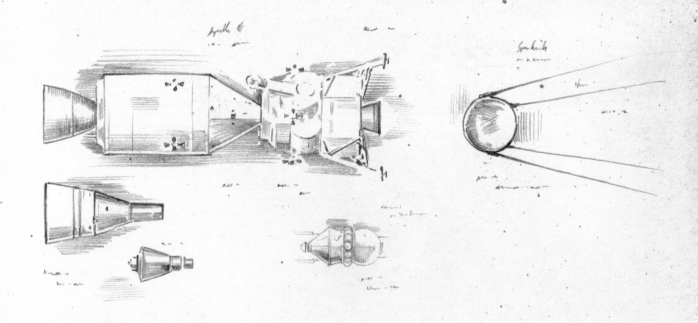

A Short History of
Space Travel

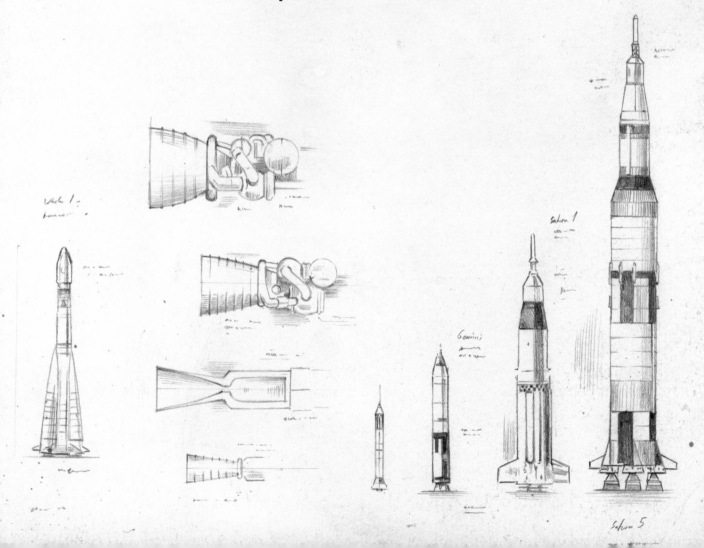

Galileo Galilei

Galileo Galilei (1564–1642) was an Italian astronomer, mathematician, and natural philosopher. He was one of the first to use a telescope in order to study the stars, moon, and planets. With the knowledge he gained, he was able to confirm Nicolas Copernicus's model of the universe, which placed the sun and not the earth at the center of our solar system. This contradicted the Church's view at the time, and his work was banned while he himself was accused of heresy. In 1633 he was forced to recant his ideas, although he is said to have murmured secretly: "And yet it moves." He was referring to the earth circling the sun. Galileo is widely regarded as a precursor of modern science.

Konstantin Tsiolkovsky

Born in Russia, Konstantin Eduardovich Tsiolkovsky (1857–1935) was one of the founding fathers of space travel. As an amateur research scientist and writer, he worked on rocket technology and developed ideas for liquid fuels and multistage rockets.

Goddard with his test rocket, 1926

Robert Goddard

Dr. Robert Hutchings Goddard (1882–1945) was an American pioneer in the field of rocket science. In 1920 he published a treatise entitled *A Method of Reaching Extreme Altitudes*. He was convinced that fully laden rockets could reach the moon. In 1925 he successfully tested a machine he had developed using liquid fuel. One year later, he launched his first test rocket. The flight lasted only 2.5 seconds, and the rocket reached a height of 13 feet. Encouraged by his supporters, who included the transatlantic aviator Charles Lindbergh, Goddard continued with his research. In 1935 his rockets flew faster than sound at a height of nearly one mile.

Goddard was only one of many scientists who worked on developing rocket engines during the first half of the twentieth century.

The First Earthlings in Space

The first space travelers, on February 20, 1947, were fruit flies. For testing purposes, they were launched to a height of 68 miles, almost reaching outer space.

A rhesus monkey named Albert II was the first space mammal, and in 1949 his capsule went up nearly 81 miles. In the decades that followed, NASA launched more rhesus and squirrel monkeys (also known as death's head monkeys) as well as chimpanzees into space. There were some mice too among those early space travelers.

The Flight of *Sputnik*

On October 4, 1957, the then Soviet Union launched the satellite *Sputnik*, thus giving birth to the space age.

It was the first time an object had been able to circle the earth. The satellite sent out a beeping signal, which was received all over the world. After more than ninety days, *Sputnik* burned up when it reentered the earth's atmosphere.

Laika the dog

The first earthling to orbit the earth was a three-year-old dog named Laika. On November 3, 1957, just one month after *Sputnik I*, she was launched into space from the Soviet Union on board space capsule *Sputnik II*.

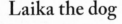

Yuri Gagarin

Yuri Alekseyevich Gagarin was a Russian cosmonaut who was the first man to fly into space. On April 12, 1961, he was launched with the Soviet rocket *Vostok I*, and orbited the earth in one minute, forty-six seconds. His space capsule returned safely to Earth.

Alan Shepard

On May 5, 1961, less than a month after Yuri Gagarin, the astronaut Alan Bartlett Shepard Jr. became the first American to enter space. His capsule reached a height of 116 miles. No orbit of the earth was planned, as his flight was part of the Mercury program that paved the way for the subsequent Gemini and Apollo missions.

The crew of Apollo 11: *Neil Armstrong, Michael Collins, and Edwin "Buzz" Aldrin*

Neil Armstrong and *Apollo 11*

On July 16, 1969, *Apollo 11* was launched with the giant rocket *Saturn V.* This multistage rocket was more than 360 feet high and catapulted the astronauts Neil Armstrong, Edwin "Buzz" Aldrin, and Michael Collins first into an orbit of the earth and then on their journey to the moon. After three days, *Apollo 11* swung into an orbit of the moon, and on July 20, Armstrong and Aldrin touched down in the landing module *Eagle.* Six hours later—on July 21, 1969—Armstrong became the first man to step on the moon. His words went down in history: "That's one small step for man, one giant leap for mankind."

The crew of *Apollo 11* returned safely to Earth. There were five more successful moon landings before the Apollo program came to an end.

Edwin "Buzz" Aldrin, the second man on the moon

About the Author

Torben Kuhlmann was born in 1982 and studied illustration and communications design at the University of Applied Sciences Hamburg. He finished his studies in 2012 with the picture book *Lindbergh: The Tale of a Flying Mouse,* which was published shortly afterward by NordSüd Verlag, quickly became a bestseller, and has since been translated into more than twenty languages. It was followed in 2014 by the picture book *Moletown. Armstrong* is Kuhlmann's third picture book for NorthSouth, and shows his keen interest in the exciting history of aviation as well as his passion for science fiction and adventure stories.

For Kristina

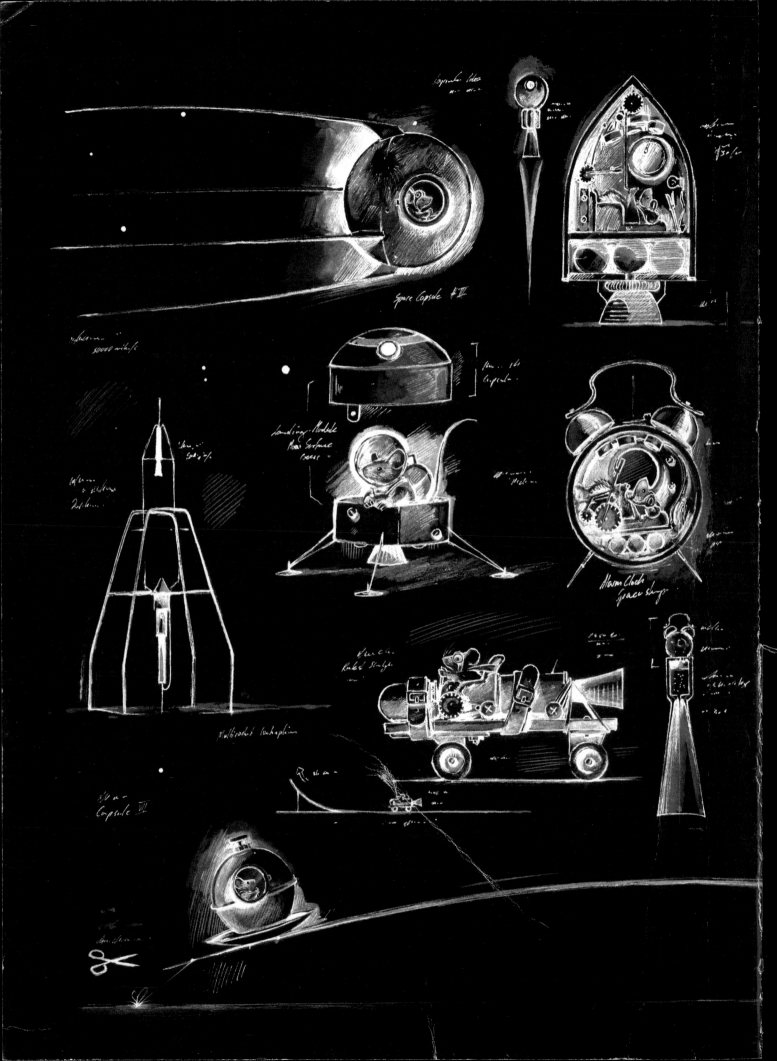